D1357711

Bing

Paint Day

by Ted Dewan

David Fickling Books

OXFORD · NEW YORK

Round the corner,
Not far away,
Bing begins another day.

Today is

Paint Day.

Here are lots of
bright colours.

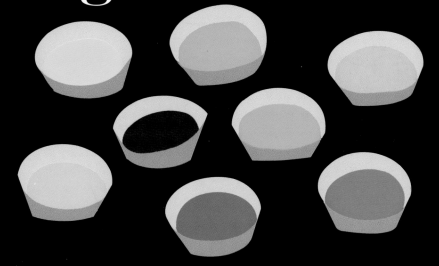

Ready to
paint.

Here is an
apron

and here is a
paint brush

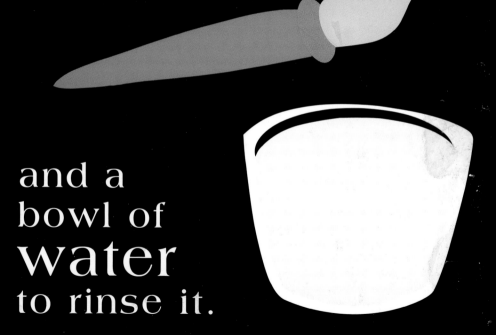

and a
bowl of
water
to rinse it.

Red

makes a cosy house.

Yellow

makes warm sunshine.

Don't spill the water, Bing.

Green

makes cool grass.

Blue
makes
the sky above.

Don't spill the water, Bing.

Pink
and
Purple

make
pretty
flowers

Don't spill the water, Bing.

Black

makes a

tornado.

Oh no! Your lovely picture!

All the colours
mixed up
and made

yukky

brown.

But never mind, Bing.

It's no big thing.

And lucky
for you,
there's one
colour left...

...your favourite colour...

ora

Paint
Day

It's a
Bing Thing.